The Three Stones Of Asche

Jake

Melissa Kriz

Dear Olivia,
Don't be afraid
to follow your
dreams!
-Melissa
Kriz

Amira Rock Publishing

Acknowledgements:

To ***Tessa LaRock***, the wonderful women who made this book possible.

To ***Andrew Buckmaster***, my editor, who gave me all sorts of constructive criticism.

To ***my parents***, who helped me figure out how this whole process worked.

To ***Athena and Erika Cohen***, for helping me see things in this manuscript that I didn't know existed.

The Three Stones of Asche

Jake

Melissa Kriz

Cover Art by: Ashley Sauer

Amira Rock Publishing
P.O. Box 5, Felton, Pa. 17322.

Printed in the United States of America

ISBN: 978-09828007-5-1

Dedication:

Melissa Kriz

To ***J.K. Rowling***, my inspiration to write in the first place.

To ***Erika and Athena Cohen***, who helped me get through the writing of this book and supported me.

To ***Alex Thompson*** for being here since I started the book and being my best guy friend ever.

And, to ***all the friends*** who never stopped supporting me.

Chapter One

OUR town is named Asche—Asche, since it is located in the hottest area ever recorded. It is our word for ember.

"I'm off hunting, Zane. Tell Dad for me!" I yelled as I walked out the door. Though I am a girl, I am the only one who can stand hunting. The others all tried, but they never had the heart to kill anything. My family felt sorry for animals and they thought deer were innocent, beautiful creatures that shouldn't be harmed. My father never realized the deer ate our corn, beans, and squash. If the deer hadn't eaten them, there would be more food for us.

In my family, we take turns hunting. I hunt on Monday, Wednesday, and Friday. My dad hunts on

Tuesday, and my brother hunts on Thursday. They never bring back meat. I usually hunt for hours, getting enough meat to last for a few days.

Today, I got up early hoping to surprise the deer before they woke up. In that case, I might not have to chase them. Catching deer is difficult. If you make any noise, they will hear you and run. You have to hang back until they stop, then try again. While hunting, I've learned you should never try to kill any deer when a buck is nearby. The buck may attack you.

I walked into the woods; and, finding the perfect tree, I climbed it and sat down. Then, I sprinkled salt on the ground. As soon as the salt hit the ground, the deer began gathering around the base of the tree.

Loading my shotgun, I aimed for a lonely deer that stood at the head of the pack. As I gently squeezed the trigger, the gun rang out with a sharp crack, and the deer fell. It was dead. I smiled to myself, thinking about my family. My dad would have put his gun down and let the deer go, and my brother would have cried at the mere thought of harming her.

Consumed by my thoughts, I didn't notice the buck charging at the tree I was perched in. The impact was so strong, I fell from the tree and badly skinned my arm. When I looked up the buck was standing there. This wasn't any run-of-the-mill buck. He was huge!

Lowering his head, the buck charged at me. I dodged, but its horns caught me in the side. It was painful—almost unbearable—and, luckily, he collided with the tree. Leaves and branches scattered everywhere.

I leapt to my feet attempting to steady myself. Panic crept along my goose-bumped skin.

Suddenly, the deer turned around and charged at me again—this time determined not to miss. I let it get close enough until it couldn't change directions, then I leapt to the side. The deer barely missed me and crashed into another tree. This made the buck very mad. He began to growl a low sinister growl that was meant to scare a grown man of his wits. I was terrified.

I took one step back to turn and run; however, somehow, I found the courage and raised my gun. My heart was pounding in my ears and I knew it was him or me. Suddenly, something made me freeze. It was a male voice. It was coming from the buck.

"Well matched, my lady," the buck stated. He scuffed his hoof across the ground and lowered his head. "I thought I had you there, but you were too quick."

My eyes widened, and my jaw dropped. I couldn't speak. Then, finding my voice, I muttered, "Is this a joke, a prank? Dad? Zane? Are you guys messing with me?"

The buck stomped his foot and flared his nostrils. "This is *not* a joke. I am the one speaking." He took one step toward me and I backed away in fear.

"You can talk…?" I asked. My mind was racing.

This can't be real. Deer can't talk.

"I can indeed talk. I am the 'Myth Bringer.'"

An abundance of ideas flooded my mind. *This is impossible! Did I hit my head when I fell from the tree? And, what was a 'myth bringer'?*

After a moment, I was able to speak. "Can all deer

talk?"

"Yes, we choose when we share our voices," the buck answered. "That is why humans don't hear us. We prefer not to share our superior knowledge with lesser beings."

"Lesser beings?" I scoffed. "What do you mean lesser beings? We keep your environment safe. If that's not smart, I don't know what smart is."

"Yes, you do try to do that. Yet, you also made cars, and they kill off deer nearly as quickly as your gun."

His eyes widened as if to challenge me.

"Cars aren't evil. They're the smart way to travel."

"They also kill us!" he shouted.

"…Well, you're right," I replied.

“Are you going to kill me?” he asked. ”If you’re not, then would you mind putting that gun down? It is very uncomfortable having that looming before my face.”

I lowered the gun to my side. “I can’t kill you now.”

“Why ever not?” He was mocking me.

“I can’t kill something that can talk.”

“You didn’t care before I started talking. You were ready to shoot me and walk away.”

“No, I wasn’t going to walk away,” I replied. “I was going to take you home and eat you. I’m sorry, but I never thought of you as anything other than food for my family. Again, I’m sorry…”

“Likewise,” he responded.

Unsure how to respond, or what to do next,

I turned to head home. I walked to the edge of the woods where I could see my village just ahead. Suddenly, a blue neon light flashed by my village and I was thrown to the ground. My hands were cut and they bled; however, ignoring the pain, I leapt to my feet and ran toward my home. I wondered if everyone was okay.

I jerked to a stop as an unusually cool wind blew across my face and I froze at what I saw. A sheet of ice had coated my town and the ice was inches from where I stood. I tried to touch the ice, but my hand went right through it. A bird flew into the enormous wall and was repelled away.

I stepped through the wall of ice and looked around. Inside, I saw my friend Mariah, her hand frozen to the doorknob of my house. She appeared to be looking for someone—possibly me.

I could also see my dad through a window: his hand was frozen to the oven. My brother's head was sticking into the pantry. And, though the situation was dire, and my day had consisted of conversing with a talking buck, I momentarily giggled at the thought of closing the door on him.

I turned to see what others were doing. The only thing I saw was the buck.

"Hello again, Mr. Buck."

"Hello indeed," he said.

"Do you know what happened here?" I asked.

"It appears that someone has removed the Three Stones of Ember." He shrugged his shoulders (as much as a deer's shoulders can shrug).

"What do you mean the Three Stones of Ember?"

"Long ago, this town was made completely of ice, and no fire or light existed. One day, a man named Vincent O'Reagan brought three stones to us—the Stones of Fire, Wind and Ice…"

"O'Reagan is my last name!" I interjected.

"Indeed it is, Charlotte."

"Hey, how did you know my name?" Creepy…

"We myth bringers know all."

"What are myth bringers?" I asked. "I thought you were a deer."

"Myth bringers delegate the responsibilities to the chosen one and help them on their way."

"Then why are you here?"

"I thought it may be obvious by now," he replied. "*You*, Charlotte, are the 'Chosen One.'"

"Me? I'm what?"

He rolled his eyes.

"You are the Chosen One," he repeated.

"So I'm going to save the town from the ice?" This was unreal.

"Yes, you are," he replied. "Anyway, the presence of the stones prevents the ice from forming. This is called the *Age of Light*. However, it appears that someone has taken the stones, leaving an open path for another age of ice."

"Why would anyone do that?" I asked.

"It is unknown to me. But, I feel it was for power. You see, your town is the most powerful in the valley. Someone must want that power."

"That story sounds familiar..." I tapped at my chin. "Hey, I know! My father once told this story to me—a story of a prophecy!"

"Do you remember now?"

Ignoring the deer, I continued, "Yeah. He told me the Chosen One was to be male though."

"He was wrong," the deer stated. "That was what the prophecy said. But, the prophecy was wrong—just as all who read it were wrong."

"If I'm to find the three stones, if they even exist, then where would they be?" I asked.

"You may want to check, Flarion, Windomino, and Glacifana," he replied. "Those towns are on the other side of the valley."

"That means I would have to go through the Valley of No Light!" My heart was racing within my chest.

"Possibly," he stated matter-of-factly.

"My uncle died going through that valley! If he

didn't live, how am I supposed to make it through?"

This was getting crazy.

"That is for you to discover."

The buck then turned and trotted away, leaving me to ponder his last words.

"*Stupid deer,*" I said to myself. "All he can do is talk. Maybe he isn't so smart after all, just too full of himself. Why would he suggest that I go through the Valley of Light?"

No matter the danger, I decided to set out on my journey. I walked into my house, taking in every detail. My brother's porcelain face was carefully searching for breakfast. His cheeks were sun burnt, matching his soccer jersey which was bright red. His shorts were quite worn, but he loved them. I remembered the day he got those shorts. It was when we had gone to the market about a year ago to get clothes. His shorts used to reach his knees. But, he'd grown a lot in the last year, so they were about six inches shorter now, a little too short.

I then turned to my father. He remained frozen as he reached into the oven. A drop of sweat had frozen to his face and his messy black hair loomed dangerously close to the burner, which lucky, was also frozen. I laughed at his stupidity for he had constantly reminded me to cook with my hair back. But, even he had his flaws. I tried to remember everything as best I could. Then, I slowly walked up the stairs to my room, wondering when, and if, I would see the town of Asche again. I couldn't stand leaving home. But in this case, I really had no choice.

As I entered my room, I remembered something

my mother had told me before she passed away. Something I only now understood.

I was seven years old at the time and she had been diagnosed with scarlet fever. The outcome was grave.

May I have a moment alone with Charlotte? my mother had whispered. Everyone in the room had gotten got up and left except for me.

What is it, Mom? I muttered, trying to hold back the tears.

Charlotte, you're special—different. You have a quest destined by fate that only you can do, and the world will rest on your shoulders. It will require great courage and strength. And, I know that you won't fail. You'll lose everything at one point, but you'll regain it later. Also, at one point, you'll give up; however, you won't give up for good. When you know your quest, enter my old room and go to my vanity. Turn the key in the lock seven times to the left and it will open. Take everything inside.

How can you say this? I asked her. My cheeks were wet with tears.

I have the ability to read one person's destiny, and I read yours. This is your life now, and your destiny.

Mom, what's my destiny, my quest? I don't understand.

In due time, you will know.

Mom, please… I need to know now.

It is unknown to me…but you will know soon. My mother's voice weakened. *You will know soon…* Her eyes closed for the last time and she was gone. I fell to my knees and wept.

After my mother's death, I promised myself

that I would never cry over her or anyone else again. But, here I was crying once more.

Sulking to my closet, I pulled out a bag and grabbed a few fistfuls of clothes and shoved them into my bag. I emptied my wardrobe in less than five minutes and glanced around my room. Without another moment's hesitation, I grabbed my pillow and sleeping bag, a few personal items, and my favorite sneakers. I then went to my mother's room.

The walls were still the same creamy orange color, and the edges were still as white as lace. I walked over to my mother's vanity and turned the key that was inserted in the lock—seven times to the left as she had instructed. The top of the vanity popped open. Several letters and a box were inside. I grabbed the letter that said READ THIS FIRST and slowly tore open the envelope. The letter smelled like my mom—a mixture of lilacs and roses. It said:

Dear Charlotte,

If you are reading this, it means I am no longer with you. I don't know how much time has passed since I've written this, but I will always love you, no matter what.

I know about your quest. You have to bring back the stones of Asche; otherwise, you will never restore the town. I know it sounds hard, but nothing in life is exactly as it seems.

The first challenge you face is in the Valley of No Light. There, you will have to make a decision. As you enter the valley, you may be made a fool of, may become arrogant and lose your wit. However, you will meet an

kind of sat there in the face of danger. It was dumb.

My mind raced. *I'm not going…But, I must… Then, finally, I will.*

The rest of the letters contained photos, and paintings my mother had painted of my quest. I only recognized one—the Valley of No Light. It was to be my first destination and it looked even worse in the pictures.

I set out imagining I would fail; and, my thoughts were only focused on making it through the ordeal. A big part of me wanted to turn around and run.

As I was leaving town, the myth bringer returned. He took me on a new path which was covered in grass except for the wagon wheel tracks that cut through to the dirt. People in wealthier towns had cars, but not us. We continued to use wagons. It was cheaper than burning gas and more traditional.

The air was humid, thick with bugs. Little red bugs, along with little blue-winged bugs, flittered around. There were also bugs with big eyes on their wings, and other bugs called 'ticks'. We didn't have this many bugs in my town. They were kind of creepy; but, it tickled when they landed on you.

After nearly fifteen minutes, we entered a large meadow. Long green grass and flowers covered the entire area. The air was fresh and it smelled like a cool spring rain. I smiled. From an early age, I loved nature. It was reviving.

I thought about my family and couldn't believe that I had left them alone. I knew it was my duty to save them, so I couldn't run away.

We walked uphill for a half an hour. Then, we started down the slope that led to the Valley of No Light. The valley was full of dense forest and heavy rain fall. It seemed to only rain on the valley and nowhere else. My mother had told me I would face a choice here: I wondered what it would be.

As we entered the forest, I heard a panther's cry followed by growls of various pitches. The cry echoed, then slowly faded away until I could no longer hear it. I trembled in fear as I took a step forward. But, I quickly found myself jumping backward at the piercing scream of another panther.

This is silly, I thought as I kept walking and glanced to the right to make sure the myth bringer was still at my side.

The sounds and smells of the forest alleviated

my tension slightly. However, dread quickly followed as another terrifying sound rang out from behind us. Slowly, we turned to face the bushes to our rear: Something was in there. And, we watched as a giant shadow grew before us.

The myth bringer and I took a step backwards. I wanted to run and hide, but I couldn't move. I was petrified.

"What is it?" I asked the deer.

"I don't know," he replied, pressing to my side.

The leaves crinkled and suddenly a squirrel jumped from behind the bush.

"Oh my gosh!" I breathed and laughed at our cowardice. "It was just a squirrel." I continued to laugh. "What an idiot..."

"Who's an idiot?" A growl suddenly rose from

behind the same bushes and a huge black panther sprung. Within seconds, he had me pinned to the ground; and, lifting a paw, he bared his claws. His fiery, yellow glare bore into my face.

"Not you!" I cried. "You're not an idiot. I was referring to me!" A faint stirring of anger lay beneath my fear. I briefly wondered where it was coming from.

"You had best not be referring to me," he growled again.

"I'm not. I mean…I was talking about me." I glanced out the corner of my eye to see the myth bringer cowering against a tree. The panther was twice his size and mine.

Suddenly, that tiny feeling of anger that was smoldering within me rose to the surface. *How could I let this happen? How could I let a panther do this to me and the myth bringer? I'm the 'Chosen One' aren't I? At least, I thought I was.*

"You're pretty brave, huh—tackling the 'chosen one.'" A mild quivering laced my voice. The anger in me was taking over and it didn't make any sense to hold back now.

"You will taste the wrath of my sword!" I abruptly shouted.

What was I saying? I had no sword. What made me make that empty threat?

"You have no sword," the panther mocked.

Suddenly, a bright light shot from my hand and a sword formed before me.

What? My mind raced, however I didn't have time to rationalize what had happened.

"I would run." The words spilled from my lips

before they were even a thought and the panther immediately dashed into the forest.

I looked at the sword that was protruding from my hand. It had turned to cold metal and a jewel sparkled in the base of my hand.

"Oh, my gosh," I whispered as I stared at it in wonder.

"See, you are the Chosen One," the myth bringer stated as he walked toward me.

I was still shaking and my mind was galloping in a hundred directions. Suddenly, another panther appeared from behind the trees.

"Don't make me hurt you," I stammered as I backed toward the myth bringer. "Because, I will!"

"I'm not here to attack you," the panther stated as he slowly walked toward me. "I'm here to warn you."

“Warn me? Warn me about what?”

“The panther that just attacked you has formed a small army. They plan on killing you. And then, they will eat you.”

“Why are you telling me this?”

“I am not a fighter,” he responded. “And, I feed only when necessary. However, the others are different. They kill for sport.” As quick as he appeared, he disappeared.

We walked on, hoping to throw the panthers off our trail. But, their faint growls which were coming from the distance, were getting closer. Suddenly, they had us surrounded on all sides. They were waiting for the signal to kill. And, they would surely eat us.

Chapter Two

"**R**un!" the myth bringer yelled as he plowed into several panthers to make a path for me.

Turning, I blindly followed in hopes of escaping. However, I was too slow and they had me completely surrounded.

"Stupid girl...," the head panther shouted. "I caught you in the woods earlier but you pulled some kind of trick and escaped. No tricks this time. Let's see who's better: my army of panthers, or the so-called 'Chosen One.'"

I stopped and looked at the head panther, my heart pounding in my chest and my hands shaking.

"You're on!" I yelled, my own words ringing in

my ears. I wanted all of the panthers to hear me, maybe the loudness of my voice and the sword I held would be somewhat of a threat and they would reconsider taking me on.

A startled look appeared on the head panther's face. He obviously never expected me to accept his challenge, however he didn't back down.

"Go!" he yelled.

The panthers came at me from all sides, gnashing their teeth and growling. I had no idea what to do or why I had accepted this fight against so many. The myth bringer had escaped and I was glad. At least one of us had gotten away.

Planting my feet, I circled slowly and watched the panthers around me. I looked for a gap or a break in the circle—something, anything—that could buy me enough time to escape. Suddenly, the panthers charged.

I'm not sure what possessed me or what made me do it, but I suddenly found myself scrambling into a nearby tree. There, I hurried to the top and scurried from tree to tree. My escape was working, I was getting away. However, a branch broke beneath me and I fell to the ground.

"Ugh," I moaned at the impact. I was convinced my body was broken and my head was an overripe, split tomato. Everything began to swim and I could hear the panthers surrounding me once more. It was the end.

"Stupid girl!" someone, or something, shouted. "I warned you to run, but you didn't."

I opened my eyes to see the panther who had warned me earlier. He quickly scooped me onto his back and was leaping to safety.

"I'll be exiled for treason because of you!" he shouted.

"I'm sorry," I stated as I clung to his neck. His stride was long and powerful and he quickly had us far from the other panthers and danger. He came to a stop.

"Now, get off," he shook to discard me like a bug.

"Ouch," I softly cried as I hit the ground. My body wasn't broken. However, I still ached from the fall from the tree.

"Thank you," I said as I stood to my feet.

"You're a fool," the panther replied. Then, he disappeared out of sight. I looked around trying to figure out where I was. I was at the edge of the forest, a clearing was just ahead.

A voice behind me immediately disrupted my

thoughts.

“You made it!” It was the myth bringer.

“Yeah,” I wearily replied. “But now, I have to rescue a panther from being killed by his own.”

“You don’t have to…”

“Yes, I do. He saved my life.”

“He’s just a panther…”

“That’s not the point. He saved my life.”

“Well, I hate all panthers…”

“You know, you’re really annoying,” I stated though I knew how he felt. My nerves were on end and my body ached.

“That’s no way to talk to the deer that’s helping you save your city.”

“Helping me save my city? You led me into that forest. You had to have known of a different way to go, maybe a way around. If that’s help, then I want to be left alone."

"You want me to leave? Let you wander the woods confused and alone?"

"Yes, I do!" I narrowed my eyes. Laser eyes, I thought. I need laser eyes! I was attempting to penetrate his skin, but nothing happened. I continued to stare at him.

"If you're going to leave, then leave already. I don't need you. I can do this all by myself."

"Fine," he remarked. Turning away from me, he trotted away.

I was dumbfounded. I didn't think he would leave. I thought he would stay and do his job no matter what. What had I done? Why was I so stupid?

I had to push all the events of the day out of my head and go back into the woods. It was so frustrating, these powers. They worked when they felt like it, not when I wanted them to. I did produce that magical sword though, which was really cool. But, if my powers only worked when they wanted, then I would have to use my own few skills. This would surely end terribly. Regardless of the outcome, I couldn't leave the panther to his doom.

My emotions were twisted, and it brought back feelings I had tried to oppress when my best friend, my true love, Jake, had disappeared a few years ago. He had been the greatest, someone I could spend my every waking moment with. And though I never admitted it to anyone, I loved him, loved him with all my heart. However, one day, Jake had found out that my boyfriend wasn't treating me right and he had confronted him. The outcome hadn't been good, and Jake was never seen or heard from again. My happiness disappeared with him.

Wiping my eyes of the tears that attempted to come every time I thought about Jake, I turned and walked back toward the forest. I needed to find the myth bringer and apologize for the way I had acted, and I wanted to help the panther who had saved me.

I took a deep breath and ran through the forest. The cry of another panther rang out and I skidded to a halt and hid behind a tree. I held my breath and peered out into the forest. It was dark.

I could see the group of panthers who had attacked me off in the distance, their campsite lit by firelight. They were enacting the sacrifice of my ally right in front of me.

"Oh, no," I whispered. I wanted to turn and run.

The panther who had helped me was hanging in a metal cage high above their camp fire. He was trying to break free, but the cage was too sturdy.

Tiptoeing, I made my way closer. If the other panthers saw me, they would probably rip me to shreds.

"I'll get you out," I whispered to the panther as I slowly began to climb the tree he was hanging from.

"Be careful," he whispered back.

Reaching the door to the cage, I lifted the latch and opened the door. The panther came sprawling out. However, I lost my footing and tumbled into the cage.

"Crap!" The hard metal door swung shut and slammed into my back. I screamed. The door was locked behind me.

"No!" Tears flooded my eyes, not so much because I was hurt, but because of the tidal wave of emotions that overcame me. I was only fifteen years old! How was I supposed to save my town when I couldn't even save myself?

"So, Charlotte, we meet again." It was the head panther's voice: It was cutting and cruel. He stood below me.

"I'm in control of the rope holding up your cage and this won't end well for you. There's no one to save you this time." He taunted me. "You will die..."

He lifted his paw from the ground, allowing the rope to fly free and the cage to hurtle toward the ground and the fire. Within a second, I would feel the heat of the flames.

I closed my eyes and thought of Jake one last time.

Suddenly, the cage was rammed and flipped over, and it landed several feet away from the fire. The myth bringer and panther had come to save me.

"I'll distract them, while you two get away!" the

panther shouted.

I was now able to reach the latch of the cage.

Lifting it, I opened the door and slid from the cage. Then, the myth bringer scooped me onto his back and bolted through the trees.

After running, for what seemed like miles, we finally slowed to a halt and I climbed off the myth bringer's back.

"Thank you," I quietly stated.

"Sure," he wearily replied.

"I'm sorry about what happened…about what I said."

"It's okay. Apology accepted," he stated.

"You know, you remind me of someone," I said to him.

"I do?" he asked.

"You remind me of someone I used to know,

but he went missing three years ago."

"Who was that?"

"He was my best friend—his name was Jake. He was the greatest thing that ever happened to me… That is, until the day he went missing."

The Myth Bringer's eyes seemed to light up, and I swore he smiled. Then, the smile disappeared.

"What does Jake look like?" he asked.

"He has dirty blonde hair, and his eyes are a beautiful blue. And, when he laughs, his eyes sparkle. I miss him so much."

What I then saw in the myth bringer's eyes was a strange mixture of fear and regret. It was as if he knew something about Jake.

"What is it? Have you seen him?" I asked.

"From his description, I'm certain that I have."

"Are you sure?"

"Positive."

Suddenly, I felt a feeling I hadn't felt in years; and, for the first time in a while, I felt hope.

"Well, let's go find him! Let's go, let's go!" I shouted with joy.

"But, what about your town?"

"What about my town?"

"We have to get the stones."

"We can do it later," I stated.

"No, we can't," the myth bringer replied.

"No one in it will know the difference; they're frozen. I bet a thousand years to us feels like one second to them."

"Yes, but anyone or anything with magical powers can enter the town."

"Anyone can enter the town?"

"Yes, anyone or anything."

I was now torn between the things I loved most—my friends and family—or my lost friend.

"How did he look?" I suddenly asked.

"Who, Jake?" he questioned.

I nodded my head.

"He looked okay."

"Really?"

"Yes. He looked fine."

"Well then, let's go get those stones," I said excitedly. "But quickly, please! Then, we can find Jake. I have to see him!"

"Sure," the myth bringer answered.

He chuckled at my enthusiasm and I laughed. It felt good to laugh, and the possibility of finding Jake rejuvenated me, gave me the desire to help my town and find the stones. We had been through so much already: I hoped it would get easier.

"So, where are we headed?" I asked.

"Flarion," he answered.

"Cool! Then, let's go!"

"No, it's not so cool."

"What do you mean?" I looked at him strangely.

"Flarion is the land of flame," he replied. "The area is covered in volcanoes, none of which are dormant. Gaping crevices blanket the ground, and if you're not wearing shoes your feet will burn." He held up his hoof.

"Oh…" I replied.

He frowned. "To put it lightly."

"I'll go anyway," I stated, determination behind my steps.

We walked for days, and occasionally we

stopped to rest. But, we hardly slept for we needed to make up for lost time. The closer we got to Flarion, the hotter the ground got. It became like a desert, like the licking flames from a stovetop. This was Flarion's defense.

Dust and dirt blew through the air and breathing became more difficult. My eyes stung and my vision was blurred. Sweat streaked my dirty face and I cursed the sun that blazed overhead. And, moving through the sand was like dragging a cement block through mud—hard. There was no end in sight.

"Myth Bringer..."

"Yes?" he answered as he coughed up sand.

"Can we stop—just for a little? I don't think I can go much farther." My legs nearly collapsed beneath me.

"Climb on my back."

"Aren't you tired?" I asked him.

"Yes, but I've had training and I know how to block it out—I know how to convince myself it's not there."

"I wish I could do that," I wearily replied.

He chuckled. "I'd almost forgotten what it was like to be…" He suddenly paused.

"Almost like to be what?" I asked.

"Never mind. It's not important."

Something flickered in his eyes and I knew he wasn't telling me the whole story.

"Okay," I remarked too tired to argue or pursue the truth. I was beat.

Climbing onto the myth bringer's back, I slung my arms around his neck and drifted off to sleep.

When I awoke, we were standing upon a gravel road and a beautiful, green oasis sat before us. The moonlight was reflecting off the cool, clear water and I slid from the myth bringer's back and stared. This land was amazing; it felt like a dream.

Within seconds, a single car siren sounded, interrupted my marveling. It was a police car barreling up the road.

"Get in!" the police officer yelled when he slid to a stop. "Now! No questions asked."

"Yes sir!" I gasped as I quickly climbed in the backseat. The myth bringer followed. "What's going on?" I whispered to him as he squeezed in next to me.

The officer overheard me.

"You aren't supposed to be in this area," he remarked. "That was the point of the desert."

"Why don't you want people coming out here?" I asked.

"I told you not to ask questions." The officer shook his finger at me. "This land is sacred to our people. We don't want intruders threatening our way of life."

I saw something suddenly change in the officer's eyes. For a second, they appeared dark and sinister.

"There's something else going on here. I saw it in your eyes."

"What are you talking about?" His tone had changed and darkness filled his eyes once more. This time, it didn't leave.

"We have to get out of here, now," I breathed into the myth bringer's ear. And, grabbing the doorknob, I pushed open the door, and jumped from the car.

"Run!," I shouted as I pulled him with me. We ran toward the lake to hide amongst the trees and the squad car veered from the road and raced toward us. The officer was laughing. But, as sudden as the dark look had come into his eyes, it vanished. Blinking, he attempted to swerve the car, but it was too late. He was going to hit us.

Chapter Three

I suddenly felt as if I was sinking, and when I awoke, I didn't know where I was. I was in a room and it was pitch black. However, somehow, I felt at peace. Where was I?

I stumbled to the nearest wall of the room and searched for a door handle or any way out. Finally, locating a door, I opened it. I was in a candy factory.

The candy factory was filled with toys, games, candy, and ice cream. It was every kid's dream. A man approached me: He appeared annoyed.

"Where am I?" I asked him.

"You're in Camtosh," he stated curtly.

"What exactly is Camtosh?"

"Camtosh is a place where people go to escape."

"Escape what?" I asked.

"Everything," he stated with a wave of his hand.

"But what about the myth bringer? What happened to him?"

"He is living out life as you left him."

"What? I left him in front of a speeding car! He would have been killed!"

"Then, I am sorry. Your friend is dead."

"No!" I shrieked. "He's not dead! He can't be dead!" I collapsed to the floor, my insides burning. A car had killed him.

"Is there a way back?" I immediately asked, unable to control the tears pooling in my eyes.

"No. Once you're here, you can never leave."

"I have to go back!" I cried.

"You can't," he retorted.

"I have to!"

"I saved your life and all you want to do is go back?"

"Yes, I want to go back! That was my life. That was my friend!"

"Well, now he's gone." He was becoming angry. "You hear that? He's gone. So, no matter what you do, he will never come back!"

I gasped as the man suddenly began to change. His skin slowly uncoiled and he was becoming a horrid monster covered in sickly, grayish skin. I now understood. This was the underworld, and in exchange for saving my life, Death had taken me hostage.

"So, you expect me to spend the rest of my life here?" I asked in desperation.

His claw-like grip was quickly around my throat. "You will remain here." Releasing me, he immediately disappeared into the shadows.

I glanced around at my surroundings. I had to get out. Lights covered the walls, and machinery was everywhere. I thought it must have taken a lot of energy to run this place, and I didn't think electricity worked in the underworld. There must be some sort of generator or power source.

I had an idea.

Tiptoeing through the maze of machinery, I spotted a door labeled, Engine Room. And, glancing over my shoulder to make certain no-one was around, I attempted to open it. It was locked. So, slipping a bobby pin from my hair, I bent it and slowly slid it into the knob. Then, I carefully twisted the pin; and, with a click, the door opened.

The room was dark, like the one I had awoke in. However, a faint light was coming from the far wall. An eerie silence filled the room, and the light seemed to grow brighter with every step I took toward it. Then, I saw it. The object was a blue crystal, the first of my town's stones.

Feeling slightly awed, I took a step forward and grabbed the stone. But, before I knew it, my mind and legs seemed to slow to a crawl. It was like being struck with a bolt of electricity. Then, the pain overtook me.

"Gah!" I cried out as I slipped to my knees and grabbed my head. It was as if my skull was being split open like a cantaloupe, and strange thoughts and ideas were penetrating my brain. Ghouls and goblins, horrid shadows and demons screamed in the darkness, and instead of being able to see in the dark room I was in, I was able to see what was happening in the room I had just come from. A portal had opened up and people were screaming and running in every direction: They were prisoners trying to break free—people that had been lured here. Armored guards fought against the people.

That portal was my only way out: I could feel it. Suddenly, the painful hold upon me broke, and I ran as fast as I could.

"Move!" I screamed at the wall of people standing before the portal. "Let me through!" The air was crisp and chilling, and it stung my cheeks. My lungs burned, threatening to fail me, and the blood pounded in my ears.

I forced my way through the crowd as the guards came

at me from every direction. However, the stone must have, by some miracle, kept me safe. An imaginary wall was surrounding me.

I could see the portal beginning to shrink. "Get out of the way!"

Suddenly, my foot struck something, and I crashed to the ground.

"Ugh!" I attempted to scramble to my feet and immediately noticed that I had dropped the stone. It was lodged beneath a large piece of machinery. So, I bent down and grabbed it. Suddenly, something hit me from behind.

"I told you, you couldn't leave here!" It was the beast who I had encountered earlier. It was Death. He had lured me here just as he had done to so many others. The portal wasn't a way to escape. It was a ploy to draw me here to kill me.

Death kicked me full force in the ribs and I screamed in pain.

"Leave me alone," I stammered.

"Die!" A man's voice suddenly yelled as his fist made contact with Death's face and the crowd of people joined in to rescue me. The stone was having an effect on them, and they were also fighting for their freedom.

Taking advantage of the situation, I jumped to my feet and ran toward the portal. And, closing my eyes, I leapt into the swirling tunnel.

"Look out!" I shouted at the myth bringer as I slammed into him, knocking him from his feet. The police cruiser sped by us and landed in the lake.

"How did you do that?" He just stared at me.

"One minute you were here, and then the next minute you were gone. Then, you reappeared and knocked me out from the path of that car. You saved my life!"

I was still shaken by the recent events. "Well…" I stammered slightly, "…When I disappeared I was being held in the underworld. Death was trying to keep me, but I escaped." I held up my hand and opened it. "I found the first stone there."

He gasped, "You did find it! I knew you were the chosen one! And, you went to Death's lair and beat him too!"

"Well, I guess…" I needed to sit down for a moment. After all that had happened, I was exhausted. I reached into my backpack and pulled out my mom's letter. New text appeared at the bottom of the paper. It said:

My Dearest Charlotte,

I guess you made it: You retrieved the first stone. Now, you will have to go to Glacifana. It is the only path you will survive on. Trust your partner. He may just save your life one day.

I was confused by my mother's words.

"What does it say," the myth bringer asked as he peered over my shoulder.

I quickly folded the letter and shoved it back into my bag. "I don't know if I can tell you."

He looked surprised. "Why not? We're a team, remember? You have to trust me."

"Trust is earned," I replied. "And, you're almost there." I smiled warmly. "Don't fret, I don't trust many people. It keeps me safer." I winked and climbed to my feet. Jake had said the same thing to me a couple of years ago. Trust me. At the time, I had and it paid off.

We had been swimming at Washwood Creek, a river just outside of my town. The water's current flowed unbelievably fast, and if you weren't careful, you could get swept away. I was never careful.

One day, Jake and I went down to the creek to swim. And, being the foolish teenage girl that I was, I went in too deep. The current quickly swept me away and I could remember screaming for Jake. The sound of the rushing water still filled my ears, and the horrid memory of me grabbing onto a log and holding on for dear life flashed before my eyes.

"I'm here!" Jake had shouted as he extended his hand to me. "Grab my hand!"

"I can't move!" I choked past the tears brimming in my eyes. "I'll go under!"

"Charlotte, you have to trust me!"

Reaching my hand out, I grabbed for his and he pulled me to safety. He was my hero.

My thoughts returned to the present. "Do you want to know the truth, myth bringer?"

"Yes, I do."

"My mother predicted this before she died and she left me letters to help guide me through my journey. She also knew something about you. Something neither of you will tell me."

"Oh," he replied.

"She also said things like: You will risk it all to save him; *and, in the end, he turns out to be the one you least expect*. "I think she is referring to you when she says that in the end—you'll turn out to be the one I least expect."

"Oh," he said again. Guilt filled his eyes.

"Tell me... please."

"No, I...I can't. That's why I couldn't say anything when I first saw you in the woods."

"Why not? Why can't you tell me?"

"It's a curse. If I tell you...I'll die."

Chapter Four

"So..." I replied awkwardly. I felt bad about pressing him, especially if it meant his death. Regretfully, I let it go.

"So, where do we go next?" he asked breaking the silence.

"Uh, maybe we should go to Glacifana."

"Why Glacifana?"

"Well, I think that after the desert we should go somewhere cooler. And, my mother had mentioned Glacifana in her letter."

"Sounds good to me," he said with that crooked twist of his lips that resembled a smile. Then, he changed the subject. "So, how did you feel about Jake?"

"I knew from the minute I met him we would be best friends," I answered. "I guess we just never got the chance to be together as boyfriend and girlfriend, to see if we were right for each other. And, after he left, I just kind of fell apart."

"Losing him did that to you?"

"Yeah." My hands were wringing. "Have you ever had someone in your life mean so much to you that you just couldn't live without them?"

"Yes, I did," he stated quietly. His gaze shifted to the ground. "I was lost without them too."

We walked for a while in silence, him in his own thoughts and me in mine. Hoping to change the mood, I asked, "So, do you want to set up camp here?"

"Sure," he answered.

We pitched a tent and gathered wood for the

fire. Then, the myth bringer went into the forest and disappeared. I waited nearly twenty minutes, and when he hadn't returned, I went in after him. I tiptoed between the trees, trying not to be heard. The myth bringer was standing ahead in a small clearing. He was eating grass.

What was I thinking? Was I afraid he had run off? Turning, I decided to head back to the campsite. However, something caught my eye and I paused.

The myth bringer was tossing his head to and fro, and acting strangely. Suddenly, he began to change. He was transforming into a human.

"What?" I blinked my eyes unable to believe what I was seeing. And, when he turned toward me—his transformation complete—my mind went blank and I hit the ground.

When I came to, I was in my tent. *Was I dreaming when I saw Jake? Was it really him?* The myth bringer stepped inside my tent.

"Good morning," he smiled warmly to me.

"But…but… you were him…and he was you… And… and…" I fumbled for what to say.

I closed my eyes in hopes of going back to sleep or waking up. I must have been dreaming? When I opened my eyes the myth bringer was still standing there staring at me.

"Aren't you going to say anything?" I asked him.

"About what?" he replied while acting as if nothing had happened.

"Ugh!" I groaned as I sat up and grabbed my backpack. I was going to get the truth…one way or another.

“I think I’m going to go to the library before we leave today. I’m going to do some research.” I knew I wasn’t dreaming. What I had seen was real.

“Don’t be long,” the myth bringer remarked. “You know we have to make up for lost time.”

Ignoring him, I headed out of the tent and toward town.

We were still in Flarion, camped just outside one of its small towns. The weather was still unbearably warm and vendors, children, couples, and other locals were enduring the heat too. It was the desert.

I couldn’t wait to get to where it was cool, Glacifana. But, I had to find out first what was going on with the myth bringer and Jake. I knew it was Jake I had seen in the forest. My heart raced with the knowledge.

The library wasn't very crowded as I walked down the various isles searching for something to explain his transformation. Finding a book on shape shifting, I pulled it from the shelf and opened it.

Shapeshifting *is a popular theme in folklore, mythology and fairy tales. It is found in some poetry, science fiction stories, fantasy books, and children's literature. It is also used in films, television, and video games. Shapeshifting, is the ability to change into another human, a creature, or possibly another entity. The shapeshifter may change at will or may be changed involuntarily by someone else. If it is voluntary, it may be done by a word, or phrase, normally associated with magic. If the change is involuntary, it may be done through a curse or a spell that has been placed on that human, either by a witch or wizard, or through other* *acts normally associated with the dark arts.*

Closing the book, I placed it back on the shelf and headed for the exit of the library. My mind was racing through the possibilities. Jake was a shape-shifter. How could that have happened? He surely didn't change into a deer on his own. So, who would have placed a spell on him?

I left the library oblivious to everything around me. I wanted to get answers. Suddenly, I paused.

A young girl, about my age, was sitting just outside the library reading. Some kids were throwing things at her, yet the girl continued to read, pretending the kids weren't there. However, after they began to throw rocks, her eyes pooled with tears and she began to cry.

"Stop!" she cried out as she attempted to shield

herself with her book.

I headed in her direction. "Leave her alone!" I shouted.

"Why should we?" the head of the group spat. "She's a freak, an empty headed freak."

"Look." I tried to remain calm, maybe diffuse the situation. "Just leave her alone. She doesn't seem to be bothering anyone."

"Mind your own business!" the leader of the group shouted at me. "She's a misfit! And, we don't like misfits!"

The girl stood to her feet. "I am not a misfit!" she cried.

The boy suddenly lunged for her and grabbed a fistful of her hair.

"Fight me!" he shouted.

"Stop it!" I screamed at him. "Stop it right now!"

The girl was thin and frail and was begging to be set free.

“It’s you or her.” The boy laughed.

“I’ll do it! I’ll fight you.” I couldn’t believe what I was saying. I knew I was the chosen one, but my powers weren’t reliable and they only surfaced when they felt like it. Plus, if I lost, who would save my town? Suddenly, the boy charged me and I grunted in pain as he twisted my arm behind my back. It popped from its socket and tears exploded to my eyes. He then threw me to the ground.

“Ow!” I cried out above the cheering of his friends as I tried to catch my breath and fight the immense pain.

“Stop it!” the other girl yelled. “Just stop it!” The boy glanced her way. This was more fun: He would beat me to a pulp. Grabbing my foot, he yanked me toward him; however, he wasn't prepared for the kick I gave him to the face. His head snapped back like a tetherball and he took a step back.

"You!" he shouted as he rubbed his chin.

I quickly scrambled to my feet and braced myself for the next attack. This time the boy charged like a running back and knocked me to the ground. Then, grabbing my ankle, he stomped on my knee. A scream rushed from my lips and I gritted my teeth to keep from blacking out. It felt as if my knee was broken.

Pain rushed from my knee to my shoulder, like hot flames blazing from a fire. It tore through the skin to my very core.

I wanted that boy to feel that burning pain too.

Fire. I could only think of fire.

All of a sudden, the boy began to scream and I opened my eyes to see him being consumed by flames. *Oh, my gosh, did I do that?* A ring of fire was surrounding me, however it didn't burn me. It was coming from my hand.

"Get some water!" someone yelled. The boy was sprayed with a nearby hose, then he took off with his friends.

"Are you okay?" the girl called to me. The fire encircling me quickly disappeared.

"I guess so," I mumbled as I struggled to get to my feet.

"Here, I'll help you." She quickly wrapped an arm around my waist to support me.

"I'm okay," I stated as I attempted to take a step.

Who was I kidding? My leg was killing me and I had to walk all the way back to camp.

"Aren't you afraid of me too?" I asked.

"No," she replied. "You came to my rescue. But, that fire was pretty wicked awesome! How did you do that?"

I sighed. "It's a long story. I'll tell you if you can just help me back to my camp."

"Sure. I'm in your debt." She smiled. She was quite pretty, and really nice.

"What's your name," I asked.

"Tera," she replied.

"So, why were those kids picking on you? Do you know them?"

"Yeah, they were making fun of me because of my father. He had gotten in a fight one day at work and lost."

I glanced at her. "Well, that's not right. Look at me, I was getting beat. People lose fights all the time."

She suddenly became quiet. There was something more.

"Well," she stated, "he died from the injuries he got from the fight."

"Oh my gosh," I whispered as a familiar stab poked at my heart. "I'm so sorry. My mother just passed away too. And, I may lose my father and my brother."

"Gee, that's terrible."

"Yeah," I stated lowly, "you have no idea."

We slowly walked back toward the campsite. It seemed to take forever.

We were silent except for the grunting that

came with each step. Nevertheless, the silence calmed me, allowed me to observe the beautiful countryside and the mild wind which was warm and inviting. It distracted me somewhat from the pain in my leg. I believed my powers were also healing my leg. I thought about my powers—how I had produced a sword then fire. What would be next?

"After I get you back to your camp, I really should be going," Tera said.

"You're going back to town? Why would you go back?"

"I don't have anywhere else to go?" She frowned.

"Stay with us. I can't bear to think of what would happen if you went back now."

"Are you sure?" she asked.

"Yes, I'm sure," I answered.

After a half an hour of hobbling, I saw our camp in the distance. Myth Bringer's head peeked up from the grass and he stomped his foot when he saw my leg.

Chapter Five

The myth bringer quickly approached us, and from the look on his face, I knew he wasn't happy. Questions began to pour from his mouth.

"Stop," I commanded him. "One question at a time."

"Okay. First off…who the heck is the girl?" he asked.

"I'm Tera Noel Fairbanks," Tera replied shocked at a talking deer. She glanced at me.

"Ok." He smiled at her, then turned back to me. "Next question: What happened to your leg?"

"Oh, uh…" I glanced at Tera then turned back toward the myth bringer.

"I was in town at the library and some kids were picking on Tera. I stood up for her and the boy that was picking on her ended up fighting with me. I ended up burning him. It was bad."

His eyes grew wide at the news. He looked at me with a mixture of horror and disbelief.

"You did what?" he asked.

"I fought him so he'd leave Tera alone, and in the process I produced fire. See…" I held out my hands, showing him the sooty spots that covered my palms. "Fire shot from my hands…"

He interrupted me. "Do you realize you could have been badly injured, or even killed? Of all the stupid, bone-headed moves to make, you chose to fight some kid in town! What were you thinking?"

"Tera, let me go," I mumbled. I wanted to run

and hide, hide from the flood of emotions that were building within me.

I hobbled to my tent, not wanting anyone to see me cry, especially if the myth bringer was Jake. The last time he had seen me cry was right before he had disappeared.

Slipping into my tent, I laid on my sleeping bag and curled into a ball. And, though the temperatures were warm outside, I shivered. Pulling a blanket over me, I closed my eyes and went to sleep.

I awoke to a tap on my shoulder. My eyes flickered open, and I rolled onto my side. I could hear myself mumbling something about leaving the campsite. I was tapped once more.

"Charlotte, wake up." It was an all too familiar voice.

"Hello?" I mumbled.

"Charlotte, it's me. It's Jake."

The second I heard his name I snapped awake. I wasn't dreaming. Jake was here!

I threw my arms around his neck unconcerned with the tears that poured from my eyes. I knew it was him, I knew the myth bringer was him!

"I knew the myth bringer was you!" I yelped, as I stared into his face. His blonde hair was cut short, and he was thin, but very muscular. His eyes were so blue.

"I couldn't continue to keep it from you." He smiled. "No one could ever keep anything from you. Plus, I'm here to help you."

"Well, what happened? Where have you been all this time?"

"I've been around." He chuckled.

"Well, why did you leave?"

"I had to. I had to leave because of the curse that was placed on me."

"What curse?" My voice bordered hysteria. "What happened to you? I know you had said something about a curse, but..."

His gaze dropped. "If I tell you, bad things will happen."

"What bad things?"

I barely heard his words.

"I will die."

My eyes widened and I clutched to his neck. I had already lost him once and I wasn't going to lose him again.

"I'll tell you someday, Char—just not today. And, seeing you crying, I had to let you know I was here, that I'm here for you."

"So, you are the myth bringer and you're here to help me? Does that mean you're going to stay? Please, tell me that you're going to stay, that you won't leave again." I gave him my best pouting lip.

"I may have to," he murmured. "I may have to leave after your quest is finished."

"Then, I'm not doing it!" I retorted. "I'm not finishing the quest."

"Char..." He took my hand. "You have to. You have to think of your father and your brother."

"Well, if you have to leave, try not to stay away too long. I've missed you."

"I'll do my best," he answered. "Speaking of your brother, how is Zane. And, how is Mariah?" Mariah was his sister.

"They're pretty good. I guess you know about what's happened with the town?"

"Yes, I do," he stated.

"Hey, then if you knew who I was, why did you attack me when you first saw me? You tried to kill me!"

"No," he replied. "If I remember correctly, you were trying to kill me. You were the one with the gun."

"Well, as long as we are together now..." I held him close. "...That's all that counts."

Chapter Six

We talked into the night as Tera occasionally stuck her head in the door of the tent to make certain I was all right. However, after seeing so many smiles, she decided to leave us alone and go to sleep in the other tent.

"Tera…" I called to her. "Jake will need that tent later and you can sleep with me in here."

"Okay…" she replied.

I smiled and turned my attention back to Jake. Truthfully, I didn't want him to leave me for a second, but I knew that him sleeping in my tent would be awkward. I giggled beneath my breath.

"You're too cute." He smiled at me.

"You think I'm cute?" I giggled again.

"A little…" His cheeks slightly colored.

I couldn't believe he was blushing on my behalf. Did he like me too?

"Well, you're cute too," I added. My face was glowing three shades of pink.

"Really?" he asked.

"Definitely!" I stated.

I suddenly got an idea. Leaning in close to him, I pecked him on the lips.

"So, what was that?" he asked.

"What was what?"

"Why did you kiss me?"

"I don't know. I just wanted to…" I responded shyly.

"Oh," he said, blushing again. Then, he asked,

"So, how's your knee?"

I was wearing shorts, so I lifted my leg and looked at my knee. It looked like it was sunburned, but it felt better.

"It's healing quickly, thanks to my powers. And, it only hurts a little."

"Only a little?" he asked.

"It's not that bad." I flinched as I moved my leg.

"You sure?"

"Yeah," I answered.

He looked me over, unsure of my answer. You couldn't hide anything from him either. I wasn't sure if that was a good, or a bad thing.

"I don't believe you," he said, raising his eyebrows.

"What?"

"I don't believe you're okay."

"Why?" I hoped to dismiss his concern.

"You flinch every time you move your leg."

"Okay. So, it hurts. Big deal."

"Now, don't be difficult, Charlotte. If it's bothering you that much and you need anything, don't be afraid to tell me."

Out of nowhere, a pain raged through my head like a mad drummer beating on a set of drums. I could see the clock tower in my town with its shiny hands and black numbers, the church steeple, the houses. In my vision, people were still frozen to the streets, and it was snowing. In all the years of living in Asche, I had never once witnessed it snowing.

The magical ice surrounding the town was flickering, seeming to be losing its power, and I could see the panthers from the valley making their way toward it.

I jerked my head up. “No!” I cried out.

“What’s wrong?” Jake asked.

“I’m not sure,” I answered. “A vision just flashed through my mind.”

“Did you black out?”

“Not exactly…” I answered.

“What do you mean ‘not exactly’?”

“I don’t know,” I stammered. “I saw our town… or at least it was a vision of our town in the future. It was snowing, and the ice covering it was broken. The panthers were headed there. They’re the same panthers that attacked us in the valley. Jake, they’ll kill everyone!”

“No, they won’t,” he said reassuring me. “We’ll

get the stones before they do."

Suddenly, I felt another jolt of pain rushing through my skull.

"Are you okay," he asked.

"I'm not sure." I rubbed my head. "All I know is that it feels like I was just hit over the head with a ton of bricks." I grimaced and continued to rub my head.

"Well, let's get some sleep." He gently squeezed me then stood. "If what you're saying is true, we have to get those stones and get back to Asche as soon as possible."

It was morning and the myth bringer was standing in the door of my tent. Tera was lying beside me. I hadn't slept well.

"Are you going to be ready to head out soon?" he asked. "And, since your leg is injured, I thought that you could ride on my back."

I smiled an idiotic smile. Even though the path ahead was going to be rough, Jake was with me, and I couldn't help but feel hope.

"Sure," I answered.

Tera quickly gathered my things for me, then collapsed the tent. And, within minutes, we were ready to go.

My destiny was set, I had found a new friend, and I was one step closer to regaining the most important things in my life. We would be headed toward another town and hopefully another stone, and whatever had happened to Jake, I would find out and fix it.

I climbed onto his back and held tightly to his neck. Pain shot through my head as another vision suddenly entered my mind: It wasn't good. We had to get moving.

CPSIA information can be obtained at www.ICGtesting.com
Printed in the USA
BVOW071554140612

292688BV00001B/2/P

9 780982 800751